Arthur and the Lost Diary

An **ARTHUR** Chapter Book by **MARC BROWN**

ARTHUR
and the Lost Diary

LITTLE, BROWN AND COMPANY

New York Boston

Little, Brown and Company

Hachette Book Group
1290 Avenue of the Americas, New York, NY 10104
Visit our website at www.lb-kids.com

Little, Brown and Company is a division of Hachette Book Group, Inc.
The Little, Brown name and logo are trademarks of Hachette Book Group, Inc.

The publisher is not responsible for websites (or their content)
that are not owned by the publisher.

First Revised Edition: January 2012
First published in hardcover in September 1998 by Little, Brown and Company

Arthur® is a registered trademark of Marc Brown.

Text by Stephen Krensky, based on the teleplay by Peter Hirsch.

Text has been reviewed and assigned a reading level by Laurel S. Ernst, M.A.,
Teachers College, Columbia University, New York, New York; reading specialist,
Chappaqua, New York

ISBN 978-0-316-11573-5 (hc) / ISBN 978-0-316-11537-7 (pb)

20 19 18 17 16 15 14 13

CWO

Printed in the United States of America

For Laurie

Chapter 1

· · · · · · · · · · ·

It was a busy afternoon at the library. Lots of people were wandering about, choosing books or doing research.

At one table, Sue Ellen was sitting alone. She didn't look up when anyone walked by, nor did she pay any attention to passing conversations. She was concentrating on writing in her diary.

Dear Diary: The library is a crowded place today. A lot of my friends are here working on school projects. Sometimes I think it's funny that I have so many different kinds of friends. I wonder sometimes why I'm friends with them and not with other people.

If I could make up some new friends, what kind would I want? Should they be friends who always give me presents or volunteer to clean up my room? Or maybe I'd like famous friends who star in TV shows or movies. What makes someone a real friend, anyway?

Sue Ellen put down her pen. That was enough for now. She loved having a diary, a special place to write down her private thoughts. It wasn't that her ideas were always great or important. But she liked putting the words on paper, where she could look at them.

She closed the diary and traced the edge of the binding with her finger. Sue Ellen had designed the cover herself. My Diary, she had printed neatly with a sparkle pen.

Underneath, she had added PRIVATE and DO NOT OPEN in large letters.

The library clock struck four times, reminding Sue Ellen that it was time to go. She picked up all the books she wanted to check out and piled them on her school notebook and diary. She tucked everything underneath her arm as she walked to the circulation desk. She had to shift her arm to stay balanced, and when she did, her diary slipped out of the pile and fell silently onto the carpet.

Ms. Turner sat at the checkout counter, waiting to help people with their books. She smiled when she saw Sue Ellen.

"That's an impressive pile. I see you're going to be reading a lot this week."

"I couldn't make up my mind," Sue Ellen admitted. "There were so many good books to choose from."

As Ms. Turner began checking out the

books, Sue Ellen spread them on the counter.

When she got to the last one, she expected to see her diary underneath.

But all she saw was her notebook.

Immediately, she searched among the other books.

"Is anything wrong?" asked Ms. Turner.

"No, I don't think . . . Well, yes." Sue Ellen looked around the floor. All she saw were two paper clips and a pencil eraser.

"I think I lost something!" she said.

Quickly, she retraced her steps to the table where she had been sitting. The diary wasn't there. Where could it have gone? Diaries don't disappear like magic. And they don't walk away by themselves.

She knelt down and searched under the chairs and tables, pushing aside feet when she had to.

"Excuse me. Ouch! Watch my fingers. Coming through."

Sue Ellen searched everywhere she could remember walking—and also a few places she hadn't. She even looked through the wastebaskets.

But it was no good. The diary was nowhere to be found.

Chapter 2

• • • • • • • • • • • •

Sue Ellen dragged herself back to the checkout counter. Her face was red, and her eyes watery.

"What's wrong?" asked Ms. Turner, who could see that Sue Ellen was upset.

"I lost my diary. I had it a minute ago. I don't understand. I must have left it here." She scanned the counter again. "But I guess I didn't."

"Books don't get lost in my library," Ms. Turner assured her. "Describe it to me."

Sue Ellen took a deep breath. "Well, it kind of looks like a book. It has a shiny red leather cover. Well, at least it looks like leather. And there are some blue sparkle letters that say *My Diary*. And under that I wrote PRIVATE. DO NOT OPEN."

"That's very specific," said Ms. Turner. "It should make our search easier. Don't worry — we'll find it. I'll tell everyone on the staff to be on the lookout."

"Thanks. I guess I'll keep looking myself. I just wish . . ."

Sue Ellen paused because she heard some laughing. It was exactly the kind of sound a girl might make if she was looking at a secret diary.

"I'll be back," she told Ms. Turner.

Sue Ellen traced the sound to the corner, where Francine was hunched over some pages.

"So that's where it went!" said Sue Ellen.

She marched up to the desk.

"Pretty funny, huh, Francine?"

Francine nodded. "I'll say. Listen to this—"

"I don't have to listen to it," said Sue Ellen. "I wrote it!" She snatched the book away from Francine.

"Hey!"

"And there's nothing funny about stealing someone's diary. I'm surprised at you, Francine. I thought you were my—" Sue Ellen looked down at the book. It was red, but it didn't have blue sparkle letters. "Hey, this isn't my diary."

"Of course not," said Francine. "It's a joke book. What would I be doing with your diary?"

"I don't know. You could have picked it up. It's red and says PRIVATE on it. I had it a minute ago, and now it's gone."

"How mysterious," said Francine. "Do you think it was stolen?"

Sue Ellen didn't know what to think. "It

was only valuable to me. I've been writing in it forever."

"I've never had a diary," said Francine. "What do you write in it?"

"My ideas, what's happened during the day. Private thoughts. It's very important that I find it, Francine. I mean, there's stuff in there about everyone."

Francine's eyes opened wide. "Everyone? When you say *everyone*, you mean *everyone*?"

"Yes, yes, but that's not what matters now."

"It matters to me," said Francine. "What have you been writing?"

"I can't talk about that now. I have to find my diary."

Before Francine could say anything more, Sue Ellen rushed off. If she didn't find the diary soon, she didn't know what she would do.

Chapter 3

• • • • • • • • • • •

"What's wrong with Sue Ellen?" Muffy asked Francine.

"She's all upset about losing her diary. It says PRIVATE on the front of it. She even thought I was reading it." Francine shook her head. "I don't see why that would upset her."

"Hmmmm," said Muffy. "Maybe she wrote something in it about you — something she doesn't want you to read."

"About me?" Francine put her hands on her hips. "But what would she write about me?"

"Maybe all the mean things you've done to her."

Francine looked surprised. "What things?"

Muffy folded her arms. "Like pushing her in the mud yesterday."

"I did not push her," Francine insisted. "She tripped."

"Right next to you, though."

"I just happened to be there. I don't push people in the mud."

"Well, you laughed."

"Of course, I laughed. It was funny. She was covered with mud."

Muffy crossed her arms. "You were standing next to her when she fell, and you laughed afterward. What if she *thinks* you pushed her?"

Francine bit her lip.

She suddenly saw a bearded doctor in a white coat sitting behind a large desk. After a knock at the door, Sue Ellen came in. She was spattered in mud.

"Do you have an appointment?" asked the doctor.

"No," Sue Ellen admitted, "but I have to see you at once, Dr. Zimmer. It's an emergency."

"Ah! And what is the nature of this emergency?"

Sue Ellen held out her arms. "Can't you tell? Francine just pushed me in the mud."

The doctor stroked his beard. "So I see," he said.

Sue Ellen consulted her diary. "That's the seventeenth time this month that Francine has been mean to me. Something must be done! I came to you because you're the world's leading specialist in mean children."

"True, true," said the doctor. "May I see that?" He took the diary from Sue Ellen and looked through it quickly.

"Ah, yes," he said. "Pushing. Laughing. Eating the fruit filling in your snack pie and

14

leaving you only the crust." He sighed. "I'm afraid your friend exhibits all the signs of acute ogre-ism."

"Ogre-ism?"

"Exactly." The doctor pushed a button on his desk, and a flickering TV screen appeared on the wall. It showed a girl screaming at other children. Then she pushed one of them down.

"As you can see," the doctor continued, "this is a disease in which the victim cannot control her meanness."

"That's Francine!"

Dr. Zimmer stopped the film. "We have been watching her for a long time. I'm afraid there's no help for her. We must keep her away from the other children!"

At that moment Francine burst in on them. She pointed a finger at Sue Ellen. "I thought I'd find you here!"

But before Francine could do anything further, two uniformed guards ran in and restrained her.

"Leave me alone!" Francine shouted.

"Sorry," said one of the guards, "but ogre-ism is very contagious. We must remove you at once."

"Besides," said the second guard, "the other children don't want to play with you. You've been too mean to them."

"But I can change! Really!"

The guards laughed.

"If we had a nickel for every time we heard that one . . . ," said the first guard.

"We would have a lot of nickels," the second guard finished up.

Then they both laughed again.

Chapter 4

• • • • • • • • • • • •

"But you have to give me another chance," said Francine. "I don't have ogre-ism."

"You don't have what?" Muffy asked.

Francine blinked. She was back in the library.

"It's a disease. Sue Ellen may have written about it in her diary."

Francine stood up and wiped her forehead. "I need a drink."

She headed off for the water fountain.

"Francine is so excitable sometimes," Muffy said to herself. "Sue Ellen probably didn't write about her at all." She paused, leaning against a shelf. "Of course, she did have to write about something. Everyday events can be so boring, though. She probably has to make up stories. . . ."

Muffy saw herself looking into a long mirror. She was dressed as a princess, in a long flowing dress with a jeweled crown on her head.

Sue Ellen was standing next to her. She was wearing a plain dress with no jewelry.

"Princess Millicenta," said Sue Ellen, "there is no one who compares with you."

"Go on," said Muffy.

"You are rich."

"True."

"You are beautiful."

"True again."

"And you are the smartest princess in the land."

"Three for three," Muffy agreed.

"You are so fair," Sue Ellen went on, "while I am just okay."

A shadow hid the sun for a moment.

"Who dares to interrupt my fine weather?" asked Muffy.

Sue Ellen looked out the window and gasped. "It's a dragon!" she cried. "A fire-breathing dragon. And it's causing big trouble in the village."

Muffy combed her hair. "What are the villagers doing about it?"

"They're running this way!"

"They are?" The princess was alarmed.

"Help us!" shouted the villagers. "Help us, rich and beautiful and smart Princess Millicenta!"

Muffy sighed. "I guess we should do something."

"Fear not, princess!" said Sue Ellen, putting on a suit of armor. "I'll handle this!"

She started clanking down the tower stairs, but after a few moments, the clanking stopped.

"What's the matter?" asked Muffy. "Why have you stopped?"

"Ooof," Sue Ellen called up. "I'm stuck in

the doorway." She gasped. "And the dragon is approaching!"

Muffy looked out the window. The dragon was on its way up the hill.

Muffy sighed. "If you want something done right, you've got to do it yourself."

She took the end of her long, braided hair and threaded it through a handy pulley outside the window. Then she lowered herself to the ground.

As the dragon prepared to toast Sue Ellen to a crisp, Muffy spritzed it with a bottle of her perfume.

The dragon's fire was snuffed out.

"Oh, princess!" gushed Sue Ellen. "My thanks! I don't know how I can ever repay you!"

"Well, this perfume is thirty dollars a bottle. You can start there."

Sue Ellen sighed. "You must be the most practical princess in the world."

"Yes," Muffy said happily. "I suppose I am."

Chapter 5

• • • • • • • • • • • •

"Hey, space cadet!" said Binky, tapping Muffy on the shoulder.

Muffy blinked. "What's that? You can't talk to me that way. I'm a princess."

Binky just shrugged. "Okay, okay. But whatever you are, you're blocking the shelf. I need to look for a book back there."

"Oh, sorry." Muffy stepped aside. "I guess I was thinking about Sue Ellen's diary. She lost it."

"Tough luck."

"It had the most wonderful story about me. . . ."

Binky looked confused. "I thought this was Sue Ellen's diary."

"Well, it is. But a diary is a good place to write about your friends."

"Really?" said Binky. "What did this diary look like?"

"I'm not sure. But it said PRIVATE on it."

"I saw a book like that," said Binky. "It was on the floor. I put it on one of the carts."

"You did?"

Binky nodded. "It's not good to leave books on the floor."

"Did you look inside it?" Muffy asked.

"No," said Binky. "Why would I? The report I'm doing isn't on anything PRIVATE."

"I know, I know," said Muffy. "But that's not the point. A diary can be very, um, interesting. People write down how they really feel about everything."

"*Everything?*"

Muffy nodded. "And everybody. I just hope we can find it."

She left to see if she could help with the search.

Binky was impressed. "Everybody, huh?" he said to himself. Keeping a diary sounded like a lot of work. Writing one didn't appeal to him. But if Sue Ellen was writing about everybody . . .

Binky reached up to get a book, but his arm froze in midair.

"That would even include me!" he realized.

Binky saw Sue Ellen sitting at a desk in her bedroom. She was writing in her diary.

Dear Diary: Today was very special. I was able to spend almost all my time with Binky Barnes, the man of my dreams.

She drew a picture of Binky in the margin. He had on sunglasses like a movie star.

He's so handsome – and strong, too. Today the school bus got stuck in the mud, and Binky volunteered to go lift up the back end. The bus driver said that wouldn't be necessary. But Binky did it anyway, and the driver didn't seem to mind.

I can tell that the other boys all look up to Binky. Who can blame them? I only wish I could get Binky to notice me. I try smiling at him a lot, but he only asks me what's wrong with my face. I follow him around on the playground, but he wants to know if I'm lost or something. I've even started bringing him extra desserts for lunch. At least that gets his attention. And I know he likes the desserts because he always burps afterward.

I'm not sure I can go on, though, without letting him know how I feel. Maybe tonight I should go over to his house and serenade him under his window. If that doesn't show him, nothing will.

Chapter 6

• • • • • • • • • • • •

"What's the matter, Binky?" said Arthur. "You look like the Statue of Liberty."

"Huh?" Binky dropped his arm like a stone.

Arthur was loaded down with the stack of books he had picked out. "Are you all right? You look a little strange."

"No, no, I'm fine. Don't forget, I can lift the back of a bus."

"You can what?"

"Um, never mind." Binky wanted to change the subject. "Did you hear? Sue Ellen lost her diary. I put it on the cart."

Arthur frowned. "Why didn't you give it back to her?"

"I didn't know it was her diary then. It was just some book with PRIVATE written across the front."

"PRIVATE?" said Arthur. "I wonder why."

Binky shuddered. "You can wonder all you want, but don't expect any help from me. I'm done wondering. See you later."

"Bye," said Arthur. He thought Binky was acting a little odd. Maybe holding his arm up like that had cut off the blood supply to his brain.

It was too bad about Sue Ellen's diary. Arthur knew that people didn't always say everything they were thinking in public. But in her diary, especially with all that PRIVATE stuff, Sue Ellen probably didn't hold back.

"Arthur, what are you doing with all those books?"

"Doing?" said Arthur. "I'm planning to take them out."

Sue Ellen looked at the titles. "Mystery of the Mummy's Curse, Eerie Canals of Mars. Arthur, I can't believe you read this stuff."

"Why not?"

"It's not good for you. Don't you get nightmares?"

"Not from reading," said Arthur. "I like adventures."

"Oh, really? Have you had any nightmares in the last week?"

"I—I guess so."

Sue Ellen folded her arms. "And have you read any of these kinds of books in the last week?"

"Well, yes . . ."

"I rest my case," said Sue Ellen. "You know, Arthur, I've been watching you very closely."

"You have?"

Sue Ellen nodded. "You're not perfect, Arthur. In fact, you're wide open for improvement. I've kept track of your flaws in my diary."

"You shouldn't have gone to all that trouble," said Arthur.

"Oh, it's no trouble," said Sue Ellen. "I keep everything organized in my diary. But I can't just write about these things anymore. I have to take action."

"What kind of action?"

"To shape you people up. I've made a list of the ways you could change."

She took a scroll of paper out of her pocket. It unrolled down to her feet and halfway across the room.

"'Number 1,'" she read aloud.

Arthur sighed. He looked around for a way to escape.

Sue Ellen stopped reading. "I know that look. Maybe we should skip directly to Number 78."

Arthur was almost afraid to ask. "What's that?" he said finally.

Sue Ellen moved along the paper. "'Number 78: Doesn't take criticism well.' Now, are you going to sit still? We've got work to do."

There didn't seem to be any way out. But as Sue Ellen went hunting for the top of the list, she moved slightly to one side. Arthur saw his chance—and dove through an opening in the bookshelves.

Chapter 7

• • • • • • • • • • • •

"Hey! Watch out!" cried one of the library assistants as Arthur crashed into his cart.

The books went flying.

"Sorry," said Arthur, picking himself up off the floor. "I was trying to . . . Well, never mind."

"Look at this mess," said the assistant. He started picking the books up.

"Here, let me help," said Arthur.

The assistant jumped back. "How do I know you won't try to tackle me again?"

"I wasn't tackling you," said Arthur. "I was just trying to escape."

"Escape? Escape from what?"

Arthur shrugged. "It's not important. I'm safe now. So please let me help."

"Okay. But just remember, I've got my eye on you."

Arthur began gathering some of the books. They came in all different sizes and subjects. One, in particular, caught his attention. It said PRIVATE on the front.

At the other end of the library, Binky, Muffy, and Francine were hunting as a team. The girls were looking through the bookcases, checking on the desks and chairs.

Binky was down on his hands and knees.

"Here, little diary," he said. "Come out, come out, wherever you are."

Francine gave him a look. "Do you really think that will help?"

"It can't hurt," Binky insisted.

"The diary shouldn't be that hard to find," said Muffy.

Francine frowned. "Unless somebody else has found it first."

Muffy gasped.

"What's wrong?" Binky and Francine asked together.

"Nothing," said Muffy. "I was just thinking. What if a big-time movie producer found the diary? She might want to make a movie about it. The movie would be a giant success. Everyone in it would be known all over the world. Wouldn't that be great?"

Francine and Binky stared at each other. "No!" they shouted.

"Look harder," said Francine.

"Much harder," Binky added.

They renewed the search as Arthur came by.

"Muffy, have you—"

"No questions now, Arthur. Can't you see I'm busy?"

Actually, Arthur had wondered why Muffy was looking under the seat cushions. He had never seen her do that before.

"I just wanted to know if you've seen Sue Ellen."

"Not for a while."

"Can you—?"

"Do I need to spell it out for you, Arthur? I'm *B-U-S-Y*. Get the message?"

"Loud and clear."

Arthur moved over to where Francine was flipping through some newspapers.

"What about you, Francine?"

"What about me?"

"Have you seen Sue Ellen?"

"Arthur, I'm not keeping track of anybody right now. I have a job to do."

"If you could just . . . Whoa! Binky, what are you doing?"

Binky had lifted one of Arthur's feet into the air.

"Just checking," he said. He put Arthur's foot back down.

"Well, leave my feet out of it. By the way, you haven't seen Sue Ellen, have you?"

"I can't see anyone from down here," Binky admitted.

Arthur scratched his head. "Why are you down there, anyway? Wait, don't tell me. I have to go find Sue Ellen."

"What's so important that you have to find her now?" Muffy asked.

"Oh, I found her diary."

Everyone froze.

Chapter 8

· · · · · · · · · · · ·

Arthur, Muffy, Binky, and Francine sat around the table. Sue Ellen's diary sat in the middle. The word PRIVATE seemed to be glaring at them from the cover.

Binky reached for it, but Arthur put his hand on the cover.

"I really don't think we should do this," he said. "I mean, would you want someone to read *your* diary?"

"I don't *have* a diary," said Binky, "so how would *I* know?" Still, he hesitated.

"Honestly, Arthur," said Francine, "don't you want to know what she wrote about you?"

"Well . . . kind of . . . I guess."

"It's settled, then," said Muffy. "Who's going to read first?"

Francine and Binky looked at each other. "Not me," they said together.

"Definitely not me," said Arthur.

"Well, I don't want to be first," said Muffy. "I know . . . We could spin the diary around like a compass. When it stopped, the top would point to one of us. That person would have to open it."

"Sounds fair," said Francine.

"Yes," agreed Binky.

"Very," said Arthur.

"So, should we spin?" asked Muffy.

"NOOOO!" everyone else shouted.

"Maybe we could just stand it on end," said Francine. "Maybe it would fall over and open."

"That would almost be an accident," said Muffy. "I like it."

They placed the diary upright.

"It looks wobbly," said Francine.

"Wobbly is good," Binky agreed.

The diary may have looked wobbly, but it didn't move.

"Maybe we're not staring hard enough," said Muffy.

Francine blinked. "I can't stare any harder. I'm getting cross-eyed."

"What if a strong wind came in and knocked the diary open?" said Muffy.

"Yeah," said Francine. "And that same wind might flip the pages. . . ."

They waited patiently for a wind to come by. They waited and waited.

"Muffy, what are you doing?" asked Arthur.

Muffy blushed. "Me? Nothing."

"There! You did it again." Arthur pointed a finger at her. "You're blowing at the book."

"Don't be silly," said Muffy. "I'm just, um, doing some breathing exercises."

Binky snorted. "Well, you're going to have to breathe a lot harder if you want to get anywhere."

He let out a very deep breath.

"And what was that?" asked Arthur.

"Just a sigh, Arthur," said Francine. "You can't blame Binky for sighing. I think a little sigh would do me some good."

Arthur crossed his arms. "Now you're all huffing and puffing. It's not right."

"I have to agree with Arthur," said Binky. "I don't think the wind is going to be enough. What we need is an earthquake."

"Not much chance of that," said Arthur.

"You never know," said Binky, kicking the table hard.

The book fell over—but it was still shut.

"Hey!" said Arthur. "That's cheating."

"It was just an experiment," Binky insisted. "I wanted to see if an earthquake would help."

"Forget the wind and the earthquake," said Francine. "Maybe we should just all read it together. That way we'll all be equally . . . guilty."

Nobody could argue with that.

Chapter 9

• • • • • • • • • • •

"My whole life is in that diary!" said Sue Ellen.

"I'm sure it is," said Ms. Turner. She had taken Sue Ellen into the staff room to console her.

Sue Ellen sighed. "And now my whole life is gone."

"There, there, dear. You still have your life, after all. As for your diary, I'm sure it will turn up. Diaries don't just vanish into thin air."

"I've had that diary ever since I was six. I started it on the first day of first grade."

"Really," said Ms. Turner.

"That was my very first whole day of school. I had never been in school that long before. When I got home, my mother helped me write down everything about it."

Ms. Turner nodded.

"We started with Circle Time. I had a hard time sitting still. And I remember staring at another little girl because I had never seen anyone so dressed up. Then the teacher read us a story. 'The Three Bears,' I think. I kept calling out for Goldilocks to be careful, but I remember feeling sorry for the bears at the end. At least I think I did. I'd have to check in my—" Sue Ellen bit her lip. "But I can't check it, can I?"

Ms. Turner stood up and rubbed her hands together. "You know, maybe instead of sitting here, we'd be better off continuing the hunt."

"What if someone else finds it first?"

Ms. Turner patted Sue Ellen on the

shoulder. "Then they'll turn it in at the desk, and all will be well."

Sue Ellen shook her head. "But what if that person reads the diary before returning it? No one besides me has ever read it."

"Now, Sue Ellen, I think you're getting yourself upset over nothing. You told me it says PRIVATE in big letters right where everyone can see it."

"That's true," Sue Ellen admitted.

"Why, then, you have nothing to worry about."

"Sue Ellen!"

Arthur and the others were coming toward her.

"We have something for you," said Arthur. He held out the diary.

Sue Ellen gasped. "Where did you find it?" She took the diary and hugged it against her chest.

"On one of the carts," said Arthur. "I was going to give it right back to you—"

"But we stopped him," said Muffy.

"Because we wanted to look inside," Francine added.

"You did?" Sue Ellen hugged the diary tighter. "But it's PRIVATE. It says so right on the cover."

"Don't worry," said Arthur. "We didn't look."

"Even though we were tempted by winds and earthquakes," said Binky.

Sue Ellen didn't understand, but she smiled anyway. "Well, whatever the reason, thank you. And even though I'm breaking one of my rules, I can tell you what I'm going to write tonight."

"What's that?" asked Binky.

Sue Ellen smiled. "That I have the best friends in the world."

Chapter 10

• • • • • • • • • • • •

As Sue Ellen was leaving the library, Binky held open the door for her.

"Allow me," he said.

Sue Ellen looked surprised. "Why, Binky, I didn't know you were such a gentleman."

"I'm not! That is, well, not usually." He looked at the ground. "And if you tell anyone, I'll deny it."

Sue Ellen smiled. "Don't worry. Your secret is safe with me."

She continued on to the bike rack, where Muffy was just getting ready to leave.

"See you later, Sue Ellen." Muffy put her

foot on the pedal—and then stopped. "By the way, I'll be home tonight if you need any ideas for stories."

"Stories?"

"You know, something about a beautiful, rich, and resourceful princess saving the world."

"Oh. Thank you, Muffy. If that comes up, I'll give you a call."

Muffy nodded and rode off.

"Oh, Sue Ellen," said Francine, running up behind her, "let me hold your books while you unlock your bike. Wouldn't want you to get hurt!"

"Um, thanks."

"Is there anything else I can help you with? I'm very friendly, you know. And considerate, too. And have I mentioned *nice*? Being nice is my best thing."

Sue Ellen looked confused.

"Well, see you tomorrow," said Francine. "Call me if you have any problems with your homework or if you just want to talk. And happy writing!"

Sue Ellen shook her head as she put on her bike helmet. She would never have expected that writing a diary would make her so popular.

She was still thinking about this as Arthur came out of the library.

"Arthur, are you sure nobody read my diary?" she asked.

"Don't worry, Sue Ellen. It's still private." He paused. "Is there anything else you want to ask me? Or maybe tell me?"

"I don't think so."

"You know, I take criticism really well. And I'm always ready to improve myself. So don't hold back."

Sue Ellen got on her bike. "I won't. You're sure about the diary. . . ."

"Positive."

"That's good. You might have been embarrassed."

"Me?" Arthur blinked. "I suppose you've written down a lot of ways I could improve."

Sue Ellen looked puzzled. "No. Actually, I said some pretty nice things about you."

Arthur blushed. "Really? Like what?"

"Sorry. My lips are sealed."

Arthur frowned. "That's not fair!"

"See you later!" said Sue Ellen, riding off.

"All right," Arthur called after her. "In that case, I'm going to start a diary of my own."

Sue Ellen screeched to a stop.

"You are? What are you going to put in it?"

Arthur smiled. "That," he said, "will be my little secret."